MARCIA

Last year, when Marcia was thirteen, she was "about bein' cute." This year, she's trying to figure out her place in the world.

Danny, her new boyfriend, is the main reason why things have changed. Although Marcia has girlfriends, this is the first time she's been close to a boy. Both of them know why they want to escape the inner city: for Marcia, college will lead to a better life than her mother's, while Danny is determined to avoid the drugs that have destroyed Jeffry, his older brother. The more Marcia and Danny confide in each other, the more important their relationship becomes.

When Danny starts pressuring Marcia to sleep with him, she is torn. She can't decide until she's sure, but if she doesn't give in, she'll lose him. How can she choose?

"Other girls [Marcia's] age will empathize totally and those a little younger will relate with understanding. . . . [This is] an issue book attuned to its intended audience."
—*Kirkus Reviews*

MARCIA

MARCIA

by John Steptoe

PUFFIN BOOKS

PUFFIN BOOKS
Published by the Penguin Group
Penguin Books USA Inc.,
375 Hudson Street, New York, New York 10014, U.S.A.
Penguin Books Ltd, 27 Wrights Lane, London W8 5TZ, England
Penguin Books Australia Ltd, Ringwood, Victoria, Australia
Penguin Books Canada Ltd, 10 Alcorn Avenue, Toronto, Ontario, Canada M4V 3B2
Penguin Books (N.Z.) Ltd, 182–190 Wairau Road, Auckland 10, New Zealand

Penguin Books Ltd, Registered Offices: Harmondsworth, Middlesex, England

First published in the United States of America by The Viking Press, 1976
Published in Puffin Books, 1991
3   5   7   9   10   8   6   4
Copyright © John Steptoe, 1976
All rights reserved

Library of Congress Catalog Card Number: 90-53395
ISBN: 0-14-034669-4

Printed in the United States of America

TO MY SISTER MARCIA

MARCIA

MARCIA

Okay, now, let me tell you about it, as far as what already went down. Most of what stays in my head is the stuff that happened last year, cause that was the beginnin. You know? I mean the beginnin of me gettin into growin up. About . . . about myself and my world. Ya-dig? Like last year I was about bein cute. I was the cutest thing out on the handball court every Saturday. I loves me some handball.

My name is Marcia Anne Williams. I live in the Brevoort Projects No. 2745, Brooklyn, New York. I go to Junior High School 33, and if you want my number you can look it up cause it's in the book.

Me and my friend Millie ride to school every morning on the train. Millie lives in my building up on the ninth floor. This mornin I was runnin late, so Millie came down to pick me up.

"Girl, you better hurry up. We gonna be late," she yelled. She was standin at the door waitin.

"I'm comin, I'm comin."

We ran down to the train station and we was almost at the turnstile when I remembered. "Oh, wow, I forgot my train pass!"

"Girl, what's wrong with you this mornin?"

Now we was runnin real late. So I just took out my little phone book and held it up like it was a pass and walked on through . . . *fast*. Boy, I was scared the man was gonna stop me. I'm glad he wasn't lookin.

We both was runnin up the stairs when the train came. We got on laughin.

"Girl, they gonna put your butt in jail," Millie said.

"Well, at least we won't be late."

After school me and my friends and some other kids from the Brevoorts take the same train home. I know them people on the train be sorry to see us comin! We be doin a whole lot of talkin and laughin and whatnot. Makin all this noise. Honey, I know the conductor be ready to throw us off the train. We be havin a whole lot of fun.

On the way home me and Millie, Evette and Paula Johasson was talkin about Mr. Goldburg, our history teacher. The man's got the breath of a dead elephant. And then at Halsey Street this fine boy got on the train. I mean he was givin you face!

Paula says, "Marcia, check out that boy who just got on, ain't he fine?"

Millie said, "Yeah, I'd like to check him out myself." He was standin there smilin cause he knew we was diggin on him.

"*Mira,* listen," says Millie. "Why don't you guys come over to my house and do your homework?"

"Yeah, how we gonna get back on the train?" Paula and Evette live two stops after us.

"Aw, girl, don't worry about it. The man in the token booth is my uncle. He gets on at three. He'll let you back on."

"Yeah, he better," says Evette. "I ain't got a dime on me."

"Yeah, you ain't got one on you or anywhere else," I said.

"Aw, be quiet."

Me and Evette never really did get along. I

don't know what it was. But every time one of us had anything to say about the other it was always bad.

"*Mira,* what you guys gonna be doin this summer?" That Millie, she always be startin off her sentences like that. I told her I don't speak Spanish.

"I don't know what I'm gonna be doin. What you doin?"

"Girl, I'm goin to Puerto Rico. . . ."

I love Millie, she's my best friend. Me and her is real tight. Like white on rice (Uncle Ben's). She's so funny. And it seems that sometimes when we be together, like we always know what the other is thinkin and sometimes we don't even have to be talkin. We just be sittin around checkin everybody out and then I'll see somethin funny and I'll look at Millie and we'll both start laughin. Just like that. Millie's all right. We all got off the train and was over to her house, up on the ninth floor.

We s'pose to be doin homework, a report for Mrs. Moore. Someone turned on the radio. I was trying on some pants.

But when I heard my favorite song, I began to dance.

4

A cheatin wife will make you mad
A snaggle-tooth chile a make you sad.
We s'pose to be up here, just studyin our minds away,
But instead we're dancin and listenin to the music play.
We was tryin on each others' clothes to see who looks the best,
Measurin with the ruler to see who's got mo' chest.
Talkin bout our boyfriends and who we gonna quit,
Talkin bout the cutest boys and who we gonna get.
A cheatin boy will make you sad
But a brand new song will make you glad.

It was gettin late.

"Chile, let me get my coat, time to go," said Paula and Evette.

I stayed up to Millie's that night. First I went down to ask Mama if it was all right. Me and Millie was talkin bout the fellas, of course. That's all we ever talk about really. I was into some deep thinkin. You know what I mean?

"Know somethin, Millie?"

"What?"

"Boys are a blip. I mean they really messed up."

"Well so is everyone else for that matter."

"That's true too. But I'm talkin about how they relate to sex."

"What you say!"

"I mean, boys, they be tryin to get all nasty with you and then don't even know what they doin."

"I understand. You want somebody that know what they doin. Right on!"

"Come on, Millie, now. I'm tryin to be serious. You know both you and I don't know nothin bout nothin as far as that go."

"I know. I'm sorry. Continue."

"Thank you."

We both laughed.

"Like they be gettin all into it and do."

"I know, givin you that Valentino effect."

"Yeah, talkin bout, 'I'd like to go to bed with you' and 'Boy, would I like to get next to you.' And really, at this point all me and them both need to get next to in bed is a teddy bear."

"Marcia, when you gonna throw away your dolls?"

"Same time you throw away yours. I still look at them sometimes. Every now and then

I'll put a new dress on one of them. But you know."

"Yeah."

"But anyway. Boys be doin all that just because somebody told them that's the way men are s'pose to act. But they ain't nothin but little boys."

"And the girls be lettin them because they want to be these only women at the ripe old age of fourteen or fifteen."

"Yeah. Oh, did you hear about that fourteen-year-old girl that had this baby? It was in the *Enquirer*."

"No!"

"No! Who did it to her?"

"Her father."

"Stop!"

"Yeah, chile, her father."

"That's a shame!"

"Ain't it?"

"Marcia, I don't believe you."

"That's what the paper say. I got it right downstairs, under my bed. I don't want my moms to scope it. She'd have a fit."

"Yeah, that's a terrible newspaper."

"Ain't it bad? Well, anyway, I don't want nobody dry-humpin all on me in some hall-way."

"Yeah, that's not the way it's s'pose to be," Millie agreed.

"I kissed a boy once."

"Yeah, who?"

"Never mind, I didn't even like him, but I did it just to check it out. Wasn't nothin to it. Moma says, 'You're only fourteen years old and the first part of growin up is growin and not bein grown.' And if I can dig myself, I'm gonna have to dig that I'm fourteen. So anyway that solves my sex problems, right?"

Millie smiled. "Run it down, girl."

"Chile . . . But, still, I wonder how you can have a kid and it ain't . . ."

Millie interrupted.

"But don't sometimes your mother be gettin on your nerves, yellin at you bout the boys you be hangin with? I mean you just be talkin or playin or somethin out in the street just like everybody else and here she comes sayin, 'Don't be talkin to them boys' or 'Don't be playin with them kids around the corner cause they're bad.' And stuff like that."

"Yeah, I know what you're talkin about. My mother always be gettin after me bout talkin to them boys around Halsey Street and sayin they bad and they on drugs and this and that and the other."

"She don't be realizin they be the same as we are. Shoot! What about them boys from over the next buildin that always be up in the hallways or on the roof all the time?"

"You mean the Nod Squad?"

We both laughed.

"Yeah, the Nod Squad. She don't never say nothin bout them. Over there takin drugs and do. Shootin up under the eyelids, and stuff."

"Marcia, she *do* be talkin bout them boys. Now, don't be tellin that lie on your mother, cause she and my mother always be talkin bout Mrs. Walker's son. And your mother's s'pose to be Mrs. Walker's best friend."

"Oh, you mean Jeffry."

"Yeah, Jeffry the Junkie."

"Yeah, she be talkin bout him cause Mrs. Walker and my mother is best friends. But my mother don't talk bout nobody as much as the people she sees *me* with. She be askin me, 'Who that I seen you with and where he come from, and I don't like the looks of him anyway.' And all that. Damn, ain't I s'pose to have no friends?"

"Yeah, I know what you mean."

We talked for a long time and then I decided to get back downstairs.

"Marcia, let me walk you downstairs. I want to check out that *Enquirer*."

"Okay." But I was still wonderin bout somethin I said before Millie interrupted me. When you get hungry, is it wrong to eat? Oh well.

Next day, test day, and boy, them was some hard-behind tests they be givin out. I have to be *usin* me some books to study for them little devils. Anyway, it wasn't too bad. Least it was the last day. My head got dizzy by the end of the day. I didn't do too much talkin on the way home. Millie was off in her own head too. I was thinkin whether all this is really worth it.

I mean school and stuff. Like all that stuff they try to cram into your head, all the dates and formulas. Things you never hear bout cept in some classroom. Some teacher givin you homework like that's all you got to do when you get home. And you're s'pose to be learnin. All you do is memorize and tell yourself it's okay cause when the test's over you can forget it all. What a drag. Why do it have to be such a hassle to get through life? I mean I'm not the first girl to grow up. They can work out all that other stuff. Why can't they work out some decent plan for a growin girl? I mean look at me.

Look at my body. I didn't look like this two years ago. And after I'm able to measure my tits, where does that leave me? I'm tellin you, boy, it's a hard life.

On Saturday I'm out on the handball court as usual with my friend Maxine Jones. We was havin a nice game till Maxine hits the ball out of the court.

"Get the ball," we yelled to this boy. He throws it back. I said to myself, Uh-oh, a man! I don't know him but I seen him before. He's Jeffry the Junkie's brother, but he don't never be hangin out with his brother. And I know he don't be takin drugs. He's real cute, too.

"Hey, you wanna play?" I yelled.

"Girl, you so mannish, leave that boy alone and serve the ball," says Maxine.

He was standin at the fence watchin us play. Pretty soon the game was over. I beat, ha, ha. He came over and asked me my name.

I told him my name was Marcia Anne.
He said he'd walk me home if he can.
I asked him his name. He said Dan.
A couple a weeks passed and we was holdin
    hands.

He was the captain of the basketball team.
He told me I was his little dream,
While sippin sodas of chocolate ice cream.
I liked him cause he liked to talk.
I liked him cause he liked to walk.
And one day on one of our little trips
I let him kiss me on the lips.
(Just once.)

And then another few months passed by and it was another whole year. And all the girls were goin with boys and I had turned fifteen and the mirror on the wall still said that I was still the cutest girl in Brooklyn. (Beauty is a thing that lasts.)

"Marcia, Maxine told me that you was goin with that boy that live round your way," Evette said. Me and her and Millie was ridin home on the train from school.

"Maxine got a big mouth. Yeah, we go together."

"Yeah, he's real cute, Marcia," Millie said. "Marcia don't even have time for her old friends any more. A case of true love."

"Don't he live in that bad buildin next to yours, where all them junkies be at?" Evette asked.

"Yeah," I said, "but he ain't no junkie. I ain't hardly messin with no dope addicts."

"That's right. Marcia introduced me to him and he's a real nice boy. He goes to Boys' High, don't he Marcia?"

"Yeah."

"You still goin with Poppo, Millie?" asked Evette.

"You know it, girl, we still goin strong."

"Better than two weeks?" I said.

"Marcia, why don't you and Danny and me and Poppo go out somewhere sometime? Okay?"

"Aw, ain't that cute." says Evette.

"That's a good idea," I said, ignoring Evette. She just jealous cause her boyfriend quit her last week.

"When you want to do it?" Millie asked.

"I don't know. Chile, I'm still tryin to get myself together for Maxine's birthday party next Saturday."

"You goin, Evette?" asked Millie.

"She can't go," I said. "She ain't got nobody to take her, ha, ha."

"Don't you worry about it, Miss Marcia, I'll be there and I'll be lookin *lovely!*"

"What you wearin?" Millie asked her.

"I'm makin this pants suit. I got the pattern

for it yesterday. It's bad. Red satin with blue trimmin."

"Yeah, I know what you talkin about. It's got cuffs and two pleats up the front," says Millie.

"Aw, I know what you talkin about. I seen that pattern. That's corny," I said.

"What you mean, corny? What you wearin?"

"Huh? Oh, I'm wearin this blouse I'm makin with . . ."

"You ain't finished that blouse yet, Marcia?" Millie cut in.

"No, I'm havin trouble with the darts. It don't fit right up top. You know how it is when you're well endowed."

"Yeah, overendowed, if you ask me," says Evette.

"Well, ain't nobody askin you, Miss Pancake-Chest."

"Yeah, well I know you ain't workin from no pattern, I know you couldn't find one to fit *you*. Your measurements defy Einstein's theory of relativity."

"All right, let's not start, Miss Ten–Twenty–Thirty . . ."

"Now, now, girls, let's not be nasty. We all know we're all lovely. Everybody's lovely," Millie broke in. "Come on, Marcia, this is our stop. See you later, Evette. Say good-by to Evette, Marcia."

"Later, Funkalene."

"Whore-galia."

"Miss Subways Nineteen Seventy."

Me and Millie was off the train as the doors closed on Evette's last comment. I couldn't hear what she said.

"Why you and Evette always fightin? You two are too much." We walked down the steps to the street.

"Aw, we don't mean it. We just be playin. Me and Evette are the best of friends, the dog fart."

We walked home. We took the elevator up.

"I see you later, girl. I gotta get in here and clean up the house fore my moms gets home."

"Bye."

My mother is a waitress around on Fulton Street and it don't take her no time to get home.

Well, Saturday rolls around and I was ready. I finished my blouse except for two buttons. It had come out nice. I surprised myself. Specially the pockets and buttonholes and stuff. I looked fine in it too. I was tryin it on, lookin at myself in the mirror in my room. Moma came in.

"Marcia, who's s'pose to be takin you to this party tonight? That Daniel Walker boy?"

"Yes, Moma." I know she was gettin ready to give me the business.

"I saw him today over at the next buildin talkin to some of them bad boys that Jeffry be with. Miss Mack says that she's pretty sure that his brother uses drugs."

"Well, Moma, that's where Daniel lives and I s'pose he would know some of the people that live in his buildin and he ain't got nothin to do with what his brother do."

"Yeah, but are you sure of that?"

"Moma, Daniel's all right with me."

"Don't be smart now. Yawl young girls are so smart, think you know everything and can't nobody tell you nothin! You get pregnant or somethin, you'll be bringin some runny-nose kid here for me to take care of. You should listen sometime. Somebody can tell you some-thin. You don't know half of what it's about. You got your whole life ahead of you. You're only fifteen years old and you're a very attrac-tive girl and boys can take advantage of you. Don't you understand, Marcia? Moma loves you and she doesn't want to see your life get messed up before you get started."

"Yeah, I know you love me, Moma."

"I just get so afraid somethin bad will happen to you. This is a bad messed-up world we're in and it's so easy for your whole life to go down the drain before you get a chance to live it."

"I'll be careful, Moma."

"Did you finish your blouse?"

"Yeah! See! I just gotta put the two buttons on the pockets."

"That's nice. Very nice. You ain't gonna wear it all unbuttoned like that at the top, are you?"

"What's wrong with that?"

"Marcia, button up that shirt like you got some sense."

"Moma!"

"Well, what you got them buttons on there for if you ain't gonna use them? Put a scarf or somethin up there."

"I ain't got no scarf."

"Well, you ain't leavin outa here till you get that shirt together up there. I ain't lettin you go out with your chest all open like that. What time that boy s'pose to pick you up?"

"Eight o'clock."

"Well, I want you back at twelve sharp; that's too late for a girl your age to be out anyway. Twelve o'clock, Marcia. I don't want to have to come lookin for you. I got to go to work in the mornin."

"Yes, Ma."

"Yes, Ma. Yes, Ma. You sayin that but you ain't listenin. It's goin in one ear and out the other. You better listen, Marcia. Somebody know somethin besides you. Twelve o'clock, Marcia, and fix that blouse."

"Yes, Ma."

She walked out and I finished my blouse. And then got ready to take a bath and get me nerves together.

At fifteen minutes after eight Danny was knockin at the door. Moma answered it.

"Hello, Mrs. Williams." He came in.

"Good evenin," my moma said.

"Hi, Danny, wait a minute. I'm almost ready."

They went in the kitchen and and sat down. Then a little later I came out.

"Good night, Mrs. Williams."

"Good night. Twelve o'clock, Marcia."

18

We left. We was walkin down the steps instead of the elevator.

"You look nice, Marcia. You make that?"

"Yeah, what was you and my mother talkin about?"

"Nothin. She was just askin me about school and about my family. Stuff like that. I didn't know you could sew."

" 'If I can sew, you can sew.' She ask you bout your brother?"

"Which one?"

"You know which one."

"You mean Jeff? Oh, she didn't say nothin bout that."

"You really like it?"

"Yeah."

When we got to Maxine's party there were a lot of people there but wasn't nothin happenin too much. They was just waitin for me to get it started.

Maxine was havin her party down in the playroom in the basement of her buildin. Everything looked nice. And everybody was there! Even Emily Dawson. Poor Emily, she's *sooooo* ugly. Wouldn't be so bad if her eyes wasn't crossed. Her eyes are so confused they git in each other's way. She was sittin in the corner at the record player playin the records, only thing she can do, ain't nobody gonna ask her to dance. Let me stop. Emily's a nice girl. Maybe I'll ask her to dance.

All the girls gasped when me and my Danny boy walked in. There go Poppo and Millie over by the table. Millie was sittin on Poppo's lap. They so cute. And there go Miss Stinkbutt over there with . . . who that boy she with?! All right! You know Miss Evette done bagged herself a man for the occasion. We walked over to Maxine and I kissed her and wished her a happy birthday.

"How's it feel to be an old woman of fifteen?" I asked. "I see you wearin my present."

I had given her a bottle of perfume and she had me give it to her yesterday so she could wear it tonight.

"Thank you, Marcia," she said, smilin. "You don't look too bad yourself, you and your man. Hi, Danny."

"What's happenin, Maxine? Happy birthday."

"Thank you, Danny. He's so cute, Marcia. Oh! Did you see Evette and her new man!"

"Yeah, I seen her," I said. "Ain't she fast? Ha-ha. Look like even Evette could do better than that!"

"Right."

"That child should go get herself locked in an abandoned refrigerator."

"Aw, Marcia. Why don't you and Evette stop. Yawl been feudin for the longest."

"I can't help it, the child just gets on my nerves."

"Yawl are too much! You want some punch?" she asked.

"Yeah, what you got in it?"

"Ha—nothin, I'm sorry to say. The butler hasn't showed up with the champagne yet, so I decided to serve punch."

Maxine handed me and Daniel two cups of punch.

"Thank you," I said. "Let me go over here and mess with Millie and Poppo for a while. I'll see you."

We walked over.

"Marcia." Millie jumped up. "You seen that boy Evette with? Ain't he terrible?"

"Yeah, I seen him, and yes he is. Where Evette dig him up from?"

"I don't know, but he *do* look a taste dug up, don't he?" We laughed. "Oh, I'm sorry, how you feelin, Danny?"

"All right, how you been?" he said.

"Fine! Do you and Poppo know each other?"

"Oh, man, me and Poppo been boys for a while now. How you doin, man?" They shook hands.

"What's happenin, man?" Poppo said. "How you feel, Marcia? You look nice."

"Don't she?" adds Millie.

"Thanks, Poppo, how you been?" I said. "I didn't know you and Danny knew each other; that's nice."

"Yeah, me and Danny been hangin out for a long time."

"All right, everybody, Marcia's here, now let's get the party goin! Old Emily just put on my main side. Let's dance, yawl!"

I grabbed Danny by the hand and we got out on the floor. You know how you feel when you feel real good and everything is right and the music is givin you goose bumps and you so happy you almost lift off the ground? You know what I'm talkin about.

"Somebody open up the window!" Millie yelled out, fannin herself at the same time. The party was jumpin! I mean we was steady takin care of business. Partyin back! Dan even asked Emily to dance a couple of times, he's so sweet. Me and him decided to take a break and go outside. (And get some air.) I went and got two cups of punch and we walked out. You could still hear the thump of the music on the outside. We walked over to a bench and sat down.

"You cold, Marcia?"

"It is a taste chilly out here, ain't it?"

I know he just asked me that so he could get his arm around me. Tryin to be slick. I let him. I let my head rest on his chest. It was better than him restin his head on mine, ha, ha. I could smell the smell of funk and Avon on his knit shirt. I never thought that would smell nice but it did. I ain't gonna tell you what we was doin out there on the bench cause it ain't none of your business. But when we got through lookin at the moon we went back inside.

We partied some more, then it was almost time to go. They was playin the last record; it was a slow one. Daniel took me by the hand, led me out on the floor and held me very, very tight. Our two cheeks were wet with sweat. He put his mouth near my ear and sang the words to the song—very, very soft.

Me and Dan was sittin on the steps in front of my buildin talkin, while I was braidin Danny's hair. It was late, and I had to go in soon, but I didn't want to. Sides, I couldn't go in till I finished.

"I want to do somethin tomorrow," I says.

"Somethin like what?" he says.

"Hold still, Danny." I don't know, somethin different."

"Like what?"

"I don't know, let's think of somethin. It'll give us an excuse."

"An excuse for what?"

"An excuse for us bein out here sittin around."

"Why we got to have an excuse? Damn, Marcia, not so tight . . ."

"Well, you don't want it to come out, do you?"

"I mean it's just nice sittin out here with you, OW! Ah, just you and me . . ."

"And the cars and the bars and the nodding junkies . . ."

"And the stars."

"Yeah, the stars . . . Dan, I love you."

"How many kids we gonna have, Marcia?"

"Kids! My God! What you wanna ask me that for?"

"I don't know . . . just an excuse."

"All right now, let's get back to our topic of discussion here."

"How many . . . I mean, what we gonna do tomorrow?"

"Let's go to the moon."

"Naw, I hear the service is terrible on the moon."

"Yeah, I guess you're right and I just remembered, I hate to ride in spaceships . . . space sickness, you know."

"How about slummin it and doin somethin on earth?"

"Earth!?! Why you wanna go there?"

"Well, cause I heard that on earth they still have places you can go and be alone."

"Really?"

"Yeah, plus, it's spring on the earth and spring is nice."

"Specially on earth. There's grass and trees . . ."

"And garbage."

"And blue skies and pink clouds."

"And people—hold up!"

"And mountains and oceans."

"And oceans! Let's go to the ocean. Let's take a boat across the ocean. A cruise around the world."

"All on a weekend?"

"Well, maybe some place close. Some place you have to take a boat to."

We looked at each other. I couldn't think of anything.

"Hey! I know what we can do. We can take the ferry out to Staten Island!"

"Staten Island! That's a good idea. You're so smart, Dan. What we gonna do when we get there? Hold still!"

"I don't know. Maybe we can take a bus out to one of the parks out there. Marcia, my neck is tired."

"I'm almost finished, just two more."

"Yeah, maybe I can borrow a few bucks from my moms."

"Okay, that sounds hip. Like it'll be fun."

He waited til I did the last braid. "There you go. It looks nice."

"Thanks. Okay then. I'll come and get you tomorrow, right? I'll miss you till then."

"I'll miss you too, Dan. Good night."

KISS

Next day Dan came to get me. But I was at the store; he waited for me.

"What's happenin, Danny boy?" I said, and walked up to him.

"Nice day, ain't it?"

"Yeah, nice day. You ready?"

"Course, let me take this milk and stuff upstairs and I'll be right down."

As I was goin up in the elevator I thought to myself, Dan, I love you.

We rode the train out to the ferry. I had never been down there before.

"It only costs a quarter?" I asked.

"Yeah, it used to cost a nickel."

"Hey! That's all right!"

The ferry came and all the people got on. I saw the people in their cars roll on at the bottom. We walked up out to the front of the boat. It was nice, the wind was blowin and the air was salty. We was standin at the railin holdin hands lookin at the city. It was a regular movie-type scene. A little later we saw the Statue of Liberty.

"Hey, that's pretty, we should go out there sometimes," I said. It was so nice. Then the boat pulled up into the dock, we got off and took the bus to one of the parks. I forget the name of it, Silver Lake or Forest Park or somethin. I don't know. Anyway, we got off the bus. Dan bought us some ices and we walked over to the park.

That was the first time I had ever been out on Staten Island. It was real different. There were people in the park havin picnics. It's real nice to be out in the grass and trees and do. While we were walkin I was thinkin about what Dan had asked me about kids last night. I guess at this point Dan would be the person I'd want to have kids with. I do want to have a family and all that. But, well, there's a lot of things you have to go through first. And as far as a family goes, the Blessed Virgin is the only chick *I* ever heard of havin kids without losin her virginity. And blessed I ain't. It's comin, I know it; Dan's gonna want to, and right now I'm scared as hell.

We walked into a woody part of the park where there wasn't any people so we could be alone. There was a picnic table near the path. It was quiet. Everything was brown and green, the green light shinin down through the leaves. Takin in the smell of fresh air and barbecue. We was both layin there quiet for a long time. Then I broke the silence.

"Danny," I said, "when we get up to go, I want to buy a balloon. One of those balloons that have that gas in it so it floats. I want to buy one and then let it go and just let it float up into the sky and I can watch it till I can't see it no more."

"Buy a balloon and then let it go? What for?"

"Because it'll be mine and then I'll let it go."

"But what sense do that make?"

"It'll be my balloon and I can do what I want with it."

"Then why let it go?"

"Because that's what happens when you give. Somethin that's yours and then you let it go. But I want it because I won't be afraid to give away a balloon. It won't scare me to let the balloon go."

Danny acted like he didn't know what I was talkin about. But I knew he did.

"What you scared of, Marcia? You don't have to be afraid of me."

But we was gettin close, real close. Soon I'd be asked to give. And even though I wanted to I was scared. So we bought a balloon and let it go and watched it till it faded away.

DANNY

Monday mornin Danny was sittin in his history class. He hadn't done his homework and he didn't even feel bad about it.

I'll probably fail the class anyway, he was thinking. His mind was wandering. He definitely wasn't into what his teacher was into. The class was discussing somethin real important like when some man stubbed his toe. And what year it happened. And who the hell cares! Danny was thinkin about his love life. His mind was all screwed up. He just wanted to get out of that classroom. He raised his hand.

"May I go to the bathroom?"

The teacher looked at him like he was insane for not bein interested in Marco Polo stubbing his toe. He went out to the bathroom and lit a cigarette.

How could she not want to? Nobody's even told her it feels bad. Don't she know how good it feels? Well, maybe she don't know. But ain't her curiosity strong enough for her to want to do it? I mean I did it before, once or twice. I'll never tell her. It was stupid when I did it. I don't know it was in me to do it. Once me and my friends were in the hallway with these chicks and we did it, to death. I didn't like them or anything and we were scared. But we wanted to just the same. And I never see that girl any more but it was still nice. It was nice and I hope Marcia never finds out about it but it was still nice. I love Marcia. It makes me feel good to be around her. I don't want to hurt her. Damn, *everybody* does it! Why doesn't she think of it as something that has to be done? She or me or anybody else wouldn't even be here if you didn't get into it, sometime or another. I mean once in a while. Everybody has to, it's a fact of life.

Then he thought of the brothers and nuns and the priest that used to teach him in Catholic school. I don't believe they don't screw. They're probably all fags. You'd probably go crazy if you didn't do it. Damn, boy, I'm goin crazy.

In his mind he imagined a man who had never had sex. The man was sweating heavily and his eyeballs were rolling around in his head. That made Danny laugh. Then he started feelin bad for thinkin the thoughts that were in his head.

Hey, what if I'm sick? Maybe I'm a sex fiend! Well, maybe I am. So what. Nobody knows what goes on in my own head. And it's nobody's business. Every boy probably thinks the same things, sometimes anyway. Girls are weird. But every *boy* thinks about it. Every boy knows about it . . . this feeling . . . every boy knows . . . but no boy knows when

31

he goes to sleep. He smiled to himself. Well, I guess this is what's called bein hot in the pants. He threw the cigarette in the toilet and walked out of the bathroom and started back to class. Damn, girls *are* weird. Still I wonder why you feel things that are right to feel and *not* sick but you can't let it out. I really don't believe I'm wrong. I really don't.

MARCIA

Next Sunday me and Dan just went to the movies. We didn't see too much of each other during the week. Danny was usually at practice for some game. And I had homework to do. Me and Millie would sit around under the pretense of doin homework, and talk about Danny and Poppo. That Sunday afternoon me and Danny went to see some dinkie picture down on Fulton Street. Sunny day, walkin down the street, holdin hands. We passed by a record shop. They was playin this song we both like. We was singin it together, walkin, holdin hands, happy and feelin fine. Lookin at the people that passed us by.

There were these two dudes about twenty or twenty-one, big. They were comin from the

32

opposite direction and diggin on me. Nudgin each other in the side and grinnin.

One of them walked between me and Danny, separatin us, and grabbed my hand.

"Oh, wow," I said. "What this fool doin?"

"You lookin good, mama," he said. "Why don't you come and go home with me?"

I guess Danny thought that I knew them, or I guess that I thought they knew Danny, I don't know. When Danny realized what was goin on, that these two dudes were tryin to give me the business, he moved forward to separate our hands.

"Hey yo! What's happenin, bro? You messin with my woman."

The other big punk grabbed him by the arm and pushed him away.

"Be cool, my man! We ain't gonna eat her, though she do look good enough to." They both laughed. They were both bigger than Danny and there wasn't nothin he could do short of gettin his arms broke. I was so mad I didn't know what to do. I jerked my arm away and grabbed Danny's hand. He jerked it away, he was mad too.

"Come on, Danny, let's go," I said.

He just stood there lookin mad. Feelin like he was just stepped on and couldn't do nothin about it. What a down! I mean, I could imagine how he felt. The two guys walked off.

"Come on, Danny."

"Damn, that makes me mad."

"It makes me mad too."

"Yeah, but . . ."

"Yeah, I know, what they did makes me feel bad too. Like you said to them, You messin with *my* woman. And they were messin with me. So why should you feel worse than me?"

"Aw, Marcia, don't come tellin me that dumb crap."

"Hey, now listen, what happened happened to the both of us. Maybe it is easier for me to say what I'm sayin cause I'm a woman, but it's cause people don't tell girls they have to protect their man. They say men are supposed to be like that. But that's a lot of crap. They say you s'pose to be the 'man' and stand up for *my* honor, but what the hell does that mean? It don't mean nothin to me."

"Well, maybe it means somethin to me."

"Well, I don't think it should. Not like that."

"Well, I guess it's just like you said, it's easy for you to say cause you're a woman. What I'm s'pose to do? Let somebody walk all over me?"

"Danny, you don't understand."

We walked across the street to the park and sat down on a bench.

"Well, damn, Marcia, I ain't no punk."

"I know that, Danny."

"I don't want nobody pushin me around."

"Okay, now, hold it right there. You don't want nobody pushin *you* around. And I can understand that. But they were pushin me around too. They messed with you for a reason different than the reason they were pushin me around. But you feel that you were the only one pushed around. It don't matter to me. I want you to know that. It's over now and I'll forget about it. But it's gonna take you a longer time to get over it than me. You blame yourself for bein pushed around and that's stupid. It wasn't your fault and there wasn't nothin you could do no more than I could do. I don't think you're a punk, Danny."

"Yeah, well, now you're sayin there ain't no difference between a man and a woman. Maybe what's been put on my head *is* a lot of crap, but it's still there."

"Yeah, I know. All that, you Tarzan, me Jane, crap. It's a lot of nonsense."

"Well, I'm still mad."

"Danny, there wasn't nothin you could do!"

"Yeah, I guess not. I'm gonna learn kung fu or somethin so the next fool messes with me I can pull his heart right out his chest."

"Danny!"

"I'm only jokin. But it would be nice. If you didn't want somebody to mess with you, you could just make them vanish and look slick doin it."

"Now you talkin bout you wanna be Super-man.

"You still want to go to the movies, Danny?"

"Naw, let's go get a hamburger or somethin. I don't feel like the movies now."

We got up and walked back up Fulton Street.

"What happens when you're in the right and somebody still wants to put you down? What you s'pose to do then? Just take it?"

"If you're strong enough, I guess so. We was talkin bout the Viet Cong in school."

"Yeah? The Viet Cong? What about the Viet Cong?"

"Well, they been fightin people for their land for thousands of years. And can't nobody beat them. They're small and they ain't got no atom bombs but they still steady kickin ass. Can't nobody beat them. And they just runnin around with sticks and knives and do."

"A parable, and on Sunday too. Well it *is* a shame what this country has done to them people."

"Yeah, this country is messed up. But the Vietnamese people are strong enough to take it, that's the strength, too."

"Yeah, it ain't about how strong you are. I don't want to be nobody's doormat because of someone else's stupidity."

"Hey, you know, that's right. If the world is screwed up, ain't no sense in us bein messed up too. Life is about life. Not doin somebody else in. That ain't necessary for *you* to stay alive. Sometimes strength means fightin or sometimes it means takin crap, but stayin alive is the thing. People should think of doin stupid unnecessary stuff as somethin that will kill them off cause it will.

"But what if you're not messin with nobody and they want to destroy you because of their ignorance? If they want to kill you, that ain't got nothin to do with life either, bein stupid to the fact that you live with a bunch of fools. Defense *is* cool. And I know it's a part of life. . . ."

"What if your defense ain't enough, like what just happened?"

"Well, I guess . . . I know that since . . . if it's all about intelligence . . ."

"Yeah, you can learn how to defend yourself. Kung fu ain't a bad idea, after all."

"It ain't. Yeah. It is too bad you'd have to change yourself to adjust to other people's stupidness. But we were lucky, I guess. We both came across a couple of jerks and we came out of it without any busted lips. So that's cool. But we can't ignore other people's ignorance."

"Yeah, you're right, Danny."

We both smiled at each other. We shared such a good feeling. A feeling like we'd accomplished something. It was beautiful! It was almost too good to be true. So we went over all the things we could remember bout such matters, bout fightin, honor, all the things that the grown-ups always say, old "sayings," that's what they were, old, and they were too old for us. We both tried as best we could to come up with somethin that might be wrong with what we had discovered in our minds. Well. What if . . . and what happens when this or that happens? And every time our own ideas about how we wanted ourselves to be stood strong. We had figured somethin out, discovered, understood. Understood just a little more about our world and most of all about ourselves because we did it together. And the night lights on Fulton Street were bright. It was dark now; we had talked so long. The lights were bright but not as bright as the stars in our eyes.

"Marcia, you a heavy little girl, and I'm sorry if before I referred to you as a possession. But you know what I meant. You are mine to be with, aren't you?"

"Yeah, I know what you mean and I am yours to be with."

"Us males put a lot of crap on you women, don't we?"

"Deed so."

"Poor things. You know what? I'm gonna give you the honors of buyin them hamburgers."

"Oh, I see, okay, but let's not make it a habit, okay? My moma ain't supportin nobody but me."

"Yeah, I see, you talk all that stuff and gonna begrudge me a lousy hamburger. Ain't you somethin."

We both laughed and walked off hand in hand into the rising stars.

All was well but sex was still on Danny's mind. My mind too. I guess he just got it together that we was gonna do it no matter what.

I mean, well it looks like he decided about it without talking to me about it. That Saturday my mother was out workin and I had to stay in and clean up. I didn't feel like goin out anyway cause I was havin my . . . Well, you see I was a big girl and once every month us women go through a thing called menstruation, (all of us cept the blessed virgin) of course, and I was in a nasty mood. I don't know why we got to get cramps and all that stuff. Boys don't get em. Well, anyway, I didn't feel too tough. The doorbell rang and it was Danny.

"Oh, ah, hi, Danny, what's happenin?"

"What's goin on?" He walked in.

"Ah, Danny, look, ah, my moms ain't home and . . ."

He said he knew that, he'd leave before she got back. "Okay?" he said.

Lord knows I wasn't ready. I mean I was real grouchy. We was watchin television and then it happened. His hands began to explore forbidden territories. He leaned over on me and kissed me and then proceeded to lay there, *on me*.

"Hey, yo! What's the plan, Dan? *Get up and now!* What you think's happenin here? Boy, you better get yourself together!"

"Aw, come on, Marcia, don't be like that."

"Come on, nothin. You must be out your mind."

"Look here, ain't nobody gonna hurt you."

"Got that right! Shoot! You say that like you know what you doin. And you don't know a bit more about what it's about than I do."

"Speak for yourself. But if you don't know, how you s'pose to find out? Huh?"

"I don't know, but I ain't into no practice runs, you know? It don't work like that. You can go practice on someone else. You can go practice on yourself for all I care."

"Well, maybe that's what you do. Maybe I will go find somebody else."

"Yeah, you go get somebody else and you know what I'll get? I'll get over it!"

"Well, maybe we shouldn't hang out together no more, either."

"You don't want to hang out, you just want to get somebody hung up, and I don't need it! So take it light, Jack!"

"Yeah, right. Later!"

That boy called me everything but a child of God. Then he walked out. Oh, wow, what did I do? He was hurt. It wasn't all his fault, he didn't know what was happenin with me. That was my fault. I saw him later that day and he said he was sorry he left mad and called me names but he was mad just the same. And I was so stupid I didn't try to explain. I was kinda mad myself. But I didn't say nothin. Nothin at all. He was so nice about the whole thing. But still he left. Left me to go home crying, livin with the blues.

Now my man Dan's done all that
he can, to try to make me understand
that it wasn't his plan to up and ran
with the beat of my heart, held in his hand.

DANNY

Danny and Poppo had known each other for a while. They didn't know each other well, they had just run into each other every now and then, and they'd speak but that was about it. Now that they were goin together with two best friends they both figured that they should get together and find out what the other was doin. Compare notes, and all.

"Hey, Danny, what's happenin?"

"Nothin, Poppo, what you doin?"

"Aw, nothin much."

Danny had just come in from playin ball in the park, Poppo was comin from his buildin. They both sat on a nearby bench and talked.

"How's Marcia?" asked Poppo.

"She's okay."

"Yeah, I saw yawl the other day on Fulton Street. I called to yawl but you didn't hear me."

"Yeah, we was goin to the movies," Danny said.

"Yeah, it was okay." Danny didn't want to talk about what had happened. It hurt him to think of the last happy night with Marcia. He knew somehow he and Marcia would get it back together again, somehow. No sense in tellin Poppo he made a fool of himself. Maybe he should have just come out and told Marcia he wanted to screw. And if she had said no then he could have just got up and tipped and said they could just talk about it later. Just got in the wind and there wouldn't be this big mess between him and Marcia. Well it's too late now. He thought to himself, I guess this time I didn't get away without a busted lip. And all just cause he was stupid about it.

"How's Marcia treatin you?"

"Fine, how's Millie treatin you?"

"The same."

They both smiled. There was a long bit of silence while Danny wondered if Poppo ever tried the same thing on Millie that he tried with Marcia. Maybe Poppo wasn't a dirty sex fiend like he was. They had started talking again. Danny asked Poppo how his sisters were. And Poppo asked Danny how his brother was and how their families were and then about how Maxine's party was and then there was silence again. They both wanted to ask each other the same question. They both sort of knew that. But neither of them knew how to come out with it. They'd just look at each other and grin and wait for the other to say somethin.

"Hey, man, I heard that Evette was diggin on you," says Poppo.

"Yeah, who told you that?"

"One of her friends, that girl she always be hangin with."

"Yeah, I know who you talkin about."

"Yeah, well she wanted me to tell you that, but I told her that you and Marcia was too tight and that she should go bout her business."

"Yeah, that's right. Ah . . . when did she say that?"

"Aw, sometime last week. You know how girls be talkin."

"Yeah."

"Well, she said that Evette was out to get you from Marcia and she probably do it cause she know that Marcia ain't givin it up and she wants you to know that she is."

"Givin what up? How she know that?"

"I don't know. That's what this broad was sayin."

"Yeah, well she must be out her mind, her and Evette both."

"Then it ain't true, right?"

"What? That Evette could get me? Naw, man, I can't stand that broad, she too stupid."

"Naw, that's not what I mean. I mean is it a lie that Marcia ain't, well, that you ain't . . ."

"Well, is Millie? Is she givin it up?"

"Well, ah, well, you know, I mean . . ."

"I know what you mean."

"Yeah, boy, ain't it a down?"

They both breathed a sigh of relief and laughed.

They both finally stopped roundin the question.

"Naw, man," Danny said, "Ain't nothin happenin. I been wantin to for the longest. I really love the girl. Well, you know they got pills and hookups for all that so a girl won't get pregnant or nothin. Well, anyway, yesterday I went over to Marcia's, I knew her moms wasn't home and I just walked in and like I didn't say nothin much. I just sort of . . . well, you know. Then she got mad and told me to tip."

"Aw, wow, man, does that mean that you and Marcia ain't seein each other no more?"

"I don't know, man. I cursed her out, man, I was hot. I don't know what to do now, I really dig Marcia, you know? I really felt bad about the whole thing."

"Wow, man."

"We'll probably get it together when we both cool off."

"Yeah, you'll get it together again. Don't worry about it, Dan. Me and Millie goin through the same thing, man. I know how you feel."

"Yeah, look, man, I'll see you later. Take it light."

"Sure, Dan. Take it easy."

Danny had felt a little better that somebody else felt the same way he did. Well, at least *someone* knew what he was goin through. But he still felt bad and then he thought about Evette. He was still hot and not under the collar.

Anyway, somethin else happened that day. When Danny got home his mother asked him to look for his brother Jeffry. Jeffry's After Care officer was lookin for him. He had called Mrs. Walker that evening to tell her that Jeffry hadn't been coming to the center. Jeffry was in a rehabilitation program from takin drugs. He was s'pose to go to the center twice a week. Danny didn't know what he was goin for, it didn't seem to do no good. Jeffry didn't talk to Danny too much about it. Danny and Jeff used to be pretty close but they had seemed to have drifted apart. It wasn't as if they didn't love each other any more, it was just that, well, when Jeffry started using drugs they just didn't see that much of each other. And whenever Danny asked Jeffry anything about what he was doin he just put him off and told him that he had better never catch Danny messin with drugs or he'd kick his ass. He felt good that his older brother wanted to protect him. But Danny didn't like Jeff putting him off like that.

Danny knew where to find his brother. Where he usually was when he wasn't out tryin to beat somebody for some money. He and his boys were usually up on the roof of the next buildin. Gettin high. Danny took the elevator to the top of the buildin and walked around to the steps. The hall smelled of piss and it was dirty and the steps were full of soda bottles that had been filled with water, cigarette butts, burned-out matchbooks, tin wine-bottle caps, and glassine bags torn open or balled up after the dope had been taken out. Danny didn't like to go up there and Jeffry wouldn't let him come up any further than the first landing. He told Danny that if he ever had to come up there after him that he should stand at the bottom of the steps and call for him. Danny walked up two steps and called. There was no answer. He hadn't heard anyone up there and he was afraid to go up. He didn't like the idea of what he thought he might see. He had seen his brother nodding before, but he had never seen him get off and he didn't want to. He was scared. He got himself together and went up a little further, holding on to the banister. He called again. His voice shook and wasn't so loud as when he first called him. He went up a little further, slowly, and then he saw his brother's shirt lying at the top of the landing. Now he knew his brother was there, but why wouldn't he answer him?

"Jeff! Jeff!"

He ran forward to the top of the stairs and stopped cold. There was Jeffry lying on the steps with his eyes half open. A syringe sticking out of his arm. Dried up blood that had run down his arm.

Danny screamed at him, "Jeffry! Jeffry!" But his brother didn't move. Danny's eyes filled with tears so that he almost couldn't see . . . He jumped forward and grabbed his brother by the shoulder and began to smack him in the face. He thought he heard a grunt come from Jeffry; he stopped when he heard it and began smackin him again, only harder. He didn't hear anythin else. He was cryin and hittin him, and finally he turned and ran down the steps. He ran down two flights and then to Mrs. Jaimy's apartment and banged on the door.

"Open the door! Open the door! I want to use your phone!"

The door opened and Danny rushed in. He ran to the phone. His eyes blurred with tears, he dialed police emergency and asked for an ambulance. He set the phone down and then sat down in the chair next to where the phone was and cried. Mrs. Jaimy had known Danny and Jeffry. Her son and Jeffry were good friends and got high together.

"Danny! Danny, what happened?" she screamed.

But Danny was still crying.

"Jeffry," he said, half crying. "Jeffry's up there, he looks like he's dead."

"Oh, my God! Oh, my Lord, Danny, Danny, you poor baby."

She held him in her arms and stroked his head and then began to cry herself.

They waited about half an hour before the ambulance came. He watched them put Jeffry on the stretcher; one of the men said he thought he was still alive, but he didn't know for sure.

"Are you the boy's mother?" the man asked Mrs. Jaimy.

"No."

"Can you get in touch with her?" he asked.

"Yes, I'll call her. This is Jeffry's brother."

"You should call her now. The boy can ride with us in the ambulance."

When they got to the hospital Danny waited outside the ward where they took Jeffry. Danny's mother came in, tears streaming down her face, and held Danny.

A nurse came up. "Are you Mrs. Walker?"

"Yes."

"Come with me."

A little later she came back and told Danny that he had done right by calling right away and that Jeffry had to stay in the hospital for a few days, but he'd be all right. Jeffry had just taken too much dope and he had to have his system cleaned out, then he could go back home.

And do it again, Danny thought.

MARCIA

The next time I saw Danny he told me what happened. He told me how scared he was. I was proud of him. That weekend we went to the movies. It just wasn't the way it used to be though. We didn't hardly say two words to each other all night.

We walked home and he asked me, "Marcia, when are you and me gonna get back together?"

"We are together."

"You know what I mean, Marcia."

Yeah, I knew what he meant, but my head was still screwed up about it.

"Well, when?"

"I don't know, Danny. Soon, okay?"

"Okay, soon. Marcia, I told you before that you don't have to be afraid of me."

"I know, Danny, I know." I hugged him tight and then ran inside.

The situation was gettin heavy. I had heard the story about Evette bein after Danny; I couldn't stand to lose my man to that . . . that, well, I had to get my head together.

Me and Millie was doin homework in my room the next day. She knew what had been goin on. I had told her, like, Danny had gone too far, like that. I didn't tell her it was half my fault. Oh, it wasn't anybody's fault.

"Yeah, Poppo tried that on me once," she said, "and I told him to go play with himself. Boys are too much, honey, I'm tellin you.

"How's Jeffry? I bet Danny musta been scared to death."

"Yeah, Jeffry's okay."

"That's good . . . Marcia . . ."

I knew she was dyin to tell me somethin. She beat around the bush till she couldn't beat the bush no more. Millie can't keep nothin to herself. "Listen, I'm gonna tell you this cause I'm your friend, but I been seein Danny with Evette . . ."

"Yeah, well, I don't care."

"Now, why you wanna tell that lie, Marcia? You know you care."

"Yeah, I guess I do but it bes that way sometime."

I thought to myself, it bes that way sometime. Yes it do, and don't it hurt? It feels like somethin you want and can't have. And you know you're gonna have to get used to it. Bein hurt. Losin somethin forever, and learnin to watch a balloon float away and not be afraid. Not let it get you down for too long after it's faded from your sight. Your balloon.

It must have looked to Millie like I wanted to be alone.

"Marcia, I'm goin now, okay? We can talk tomorrow."

"Yeah, okay, Millie, I'll see you later."

She left, I closed the door, and began to cry. I cried not because I was alone or because something had gone wrong. I cried because "it bes that way sometime."

Sometimes it's good, sometimes it's bad. Good times, bad times, that's the way it be. There's nothin to be done. It just bes that way sometimes. I know things like this are goin to happen to me again. And I'll have to go through it again. And I'll have to get over it, more than once. What a drag. I can see more of how Danny felt the day those two guys messed with us on the way to the movies. Totally helpless . . .

Next mornin on the train on the way to school, I says to Millie, "Millie, look, I want to talk to you about somethin."

"Yeah, what? Is it serious?"

"Yeah."

"Oh, wow, outa sight, turbulence. What's it about?"

"Millie, come on. I'll tell you after school."

"Oh, it *is* serious, I'm sorry. We'll do our homework over my house tonight. Okay? Hey, you and Danny ain't havin problems again, are you?"

"Well . . ."

"Oh, you poor baby. Okay, we'll meet after school. Okay? Oh, I can't wait."

Me and Millie never talked to each other about our sex lives. We always talked as if it was understood we were doin somethin. After school me and Millie went to her house. We got in her room, she told her little sister to get out, then she locked the door behind us and pulled down the shade and sat down on the bed.

"Okay, honey, dish me the dirt."

"Well . . ."

"Come on, Marcia, dish, dish, I'm dyin!"

"Ah, come on, Millie, I'm tryin to be serious."

"Okay, I'm sorry. You want a soda? Take off your jacket. Tell me!"

"Well, what did you do when Poppo tried to . . . did you . . . ?"

"Oh, my goodness! You didn't! Oh, you poor thing! My best friend has gone and lost her virginity. Tell me how it happened. How was it? I want to know everything."

"Millie, stop! Me and Danny didn't screw."

"Oh?"

"Not yet. I mean, I want to but I'm scared."

"Oh . . . oh! Marcia, this is beautiful. Oh, I mean it's terrible, but, at last, somebody I can talk to . . . I mean, girl, I've been out of my mind. I can't put Poppo off any longer, he's gonna quit me."

"You mean the same things been happenin to you and Poppo?"

"Yes, oh my God, too much!"

We both laughed and looked at each other and said, "Oh, you poor thing," at the same time.

"Oh, you first, Marcia."

"Well, me and Danny were gettin so close. I

mean we been makin out and do. Well, you know what's been happenin. And, well, I really, really love him. I really do. But I'm scared to do it. I mean there ain't nothin wrong with it when you're ready. But I don't want to mess up and have a kid or somethin. I mean we can't get married or nothin. I know Danny would marry me if it did happen, but I don't want to do that to him or myself. I definitely don't want it to happen to me. Like, what would happen if we did it and then broke up? People change. I mean, I don't believe in all that fairy-tale stuff about waitin till you get married to learn how to screw. I mean, that's how it was when my mother was a kid. Oh, my mother would kill me if she knew how I felt."

"Kill, chile, my mother would do worse than that if *she* knew. Oh, Marcia, the same thing's been happenin to me. Poppo told me that we was gonna have to split if I didn't get it together. I mean, I don't think he's gonna do it but I just be givin him these lines like, 'later,' or, 'we'll do it tomorrow.' And he know I'm lyin to him. And he just gets mad and says he's gonna leave me if somethin don't happen. Well, damn, I don't blame him. Who wants to sit around and kiss for the rest of their lives?"

"Oh, wow, I don't know what to do. And like, I really think I'm ready to at least check it out. But I'm just scared it will turn out bad."

"Yeah, Poppo says I can use some protection, if I was uptight."

"Yeah, I was thinkin about that."

"The pill is s'pose to be good."

"Yeah, but it makes a lot of girls sick and they can't take it, plus you never know what those things will do to your kids when you do have em."

"Yeah, we'd probably have to go through a lot of mess to get em. We'd probably have to get our mothers' permission and do."

"Yeah, and you have to take em all the time. What would happen if your mother found them?"

"Yeah, what about a diaphragm? I know some girls that went to the clinic and got fitted for one and their mothers never knew a thing. They didn't even have to give their real name."

"Yeah, I was thinkin about that, too."

"But I don't know."

"Yeah, scary, ain't it?"

"Yeah."

"Well, I'm gonna do somethin. I can't stand it no more. I wanna do it."

"Me too."

"But like, don't you have to be a certain age before you get it?" I asked.

"I don't know. Maybe we can lie about our ages. Oh, Marcia, you could do it easy, you look old enough."

"Yeah, I guess so. Good, let's do it. We can at least try."

"Good, we can go one day next week."

"Yeah, good. Millie, you're the best friend anybody ever had."

But I still wasn't sure about it. I thought, Well, I don't know, we'll see.

You know, it's funny how I'm feelin screwed up about all this and I ain't said nothin to my mother about it. It's funny, I mean usually when I have a bad cold or just don't feel good I can always run to Mommy. I wonder why I feel funny about goin to her now? She'd understand. She'd know what to do. She must have gone through the same thing. She's a woman too. It was different when I fell and hurt myself and went cryin to her. I was her little girl and she was my mommy. But now I'm not a little girl. She's still my mommy, but now I'm a woman too. That must be it. Hey, that means a whole new way between us. Two women. I'm afraid she won't be ready to give up her little girl. But it's gonna have to happen. I mean, I'm not a baby any more. Oh, I hope she understands. I love her. I want to tell her how glad I am that I'm growin up. I feel good about it now. I'm proud of what I am, of what I feel. She should know. I hope it doesn't make her feel bad. I'll always love her no matter what and I hope she'll always love me. Even if I'm not a little girl any more.

I was in my room. I heard Moma come in. Well, I guess now is as good a time as any. I walked out to the kitchen. Moma was gettin settled into the house.

"Hi, Marcia."

"Hi, Moma."

"Girl, your moma is tired, you hear me; I been standin on my feet all day long."

"You want me to cook dinner?"

"No thank you, baby. I don't want nothin myself. But you should get somethin for yourself. I'm just gonna sit here for a little while and let me feet cool off. I sure do wish these people would get that elevator together."

"It wasn't workin when you came up?"

"Naw, they didn't fix that movin piss box yet."

"It was workin when me and Millie came up."

"It was?"

"Yeah."

"Humm . . . Well, you gonna eat? You should eat the rest of that potato salad in there before it spoils."

"Naw, I ain't gonna eat either."

"Why?"

"I don't know, I just don't feel like it. You want me to go get you the paper?"

"No thank you, baby. I got one already, somebody left it on the counter this mornin. Get it for me, it's in my bag."

I got the paper and handed it to her and then sat down at the table across from her.

"Ma, I want to talk to you."

"What's the matter?" She was thumbin through the paper.

"Ma, I got the blues."

"What's wrong?"

"Well, it's about me and Danny. Well, we . . ."

"Marcia, did you go to bed with that boy?" She was still lookin at the paper. I guess she thought I was gonna tell her I was pregnant or somethin and she didn't want to hear that.

"No, we didn't go to bed." I guessed she was

relieved to hear that; she put the paper down and looked up at me.

"You sure?"

"Never more sure of anything in my life."

"Then what's the matter? Did yawl fight?"

"Yeah, I mean, we still together and all but . . . Well, it's really not about me and Danny. It's about me."

"Yeah, I know. I seen you mopin around here like the world was comin to an end. I was wonderin when you was gonna say somethin."

"Well, why didn't you ask me what was the matter?"

"Well, you know it's hard to ask somebody somethin you scared of hearin. You know?"

"Moma, I want to know what I should do. Well, what do you feel about abortions?"

"Abortions!! Marcia, I thought you told me . . ."

"Moma, take it easy! I don't need one. I just want to know how you feel about them. Jesus."

"Well."

"Well . . . how do you feel about em?"

"Well, I feel that if a young girl that don't know nothin bout life and ain't got nothin but her black behind and her hand to scratch it. And if she should happen to be runnin around with some young boy in the same position she's in and can't support no family and her moma don't want to support all three of them when she got enough on her hands as it is, I guess it would be better to get an abortion instead of bringin some poor child into the world that ain't got nothin to do with all that anyway."

"Well, now, that's what I was thinkin too . . ."

"Marcia, you said you ain't pregnant, now I know if that's what you tell me . . ."

"I ain't! But what you say about bringin a kid into this messed-up world, I mean, I agree with that, but . . . well, I been thinkin about just what's goin on . . ."

"Well, Lord, I guess my baby done growed up. I've been puttin it off and puttin it off. Well, I guess I got to face the facts . . . Moma's take you down to the doctor's and he'll find out the best kind a contraceptive for you to use."

"But, Ma . . ."

"No, that's all right, I know what you were gonna ask me and Moma's proud of you that you come and talked with me before something bad happened."

"But Ma! That's not what I wanted to . . . Oh? You will? Oh, good. But Ma, that's not what I wanted to talk about . . . You sure you won't change your mind, will you?"

"No, I've been makin up my mind."

"That's nice, Ma, I'm glad, but you know like you say, 'doin it before somethin bad happens.' Moma, I don't believe babies are bad."

"Marcia, you know what I mean."

"Yeah, I know what you mean and I also know what you said. You said babies are bad. And I don't ever want to feel one way about them and then go and say somethin like they bad. Or that I shouldn't have one."

"Well, you shouldn't."

"No, Ma, you see that's what I'm sayin. The truth is that I *can't* have a baby, but that doesn't mean I shouldn't. I am a woman. Why should a woman ever be put in a position where she don't want her children from a man that she loves?"

"Marcia, you're still young. You'd be tied down by a baby. You wouldn't get a chance to do somethin good with your life."

"Moma, I ain't gonna let nothin keep me from bein what I want to be. That would be wrong."

"Okay, you say you want to go to college and then get a good job. Who's gonna take care of your child while you runnin around gettin degrees?"

"Moma, if I get a chance maybe I could work

it out. I certainly won't be the first woman to do it. And I won't blame my baby for bein alive. I don't want to give my baby nothin but life and if I can't do it then there's plenty of people who want kids cause they can't have them themself. Besides, I got Danny."

"Can't nobody tell you kids nothin. What if Danny leaves you and s'pose you couldn't take care a kid in a couple of years? A child should have a father. Now try and tell me bout that! Tell me about bringin up a child by yourself in a place like this. I wouldn't wish that on nobody, especially not you."

"Moma, I know you love me and I know that even though Daddy left that you love him. I don't blame Daddy. I know from what you told me that he probably would of stayed if he could. You know he didn't leave cause he hated me and I don't think he hated you. If he left it was probably cause this world is so messed up that a man sometimes can't always stay with a woman. I've watched enough TV to know that TV shows aren't what life's about."

"And you still don't know what it's about. If the Good Lord wanted children to grow up without fathers he would have made it that way."

"If the Good Lord didn't want me to have kids he wouldn't have given me the power to have them. If the Good Lord didn't want me to have em this young he'd of made it so a woman wouldn't have a kid until she brought him a note sayin that she's been married and her husband's had a good job for so many years and now dear God may I be a complete woman? It's *not* God's fault that people are screwed up. He didn't mean for a woman to have to depend on a paycheck and a nice apartment in a good neighborhood before a child could be born. People were here long before all that crap existed. I will *not* have my life and my child's life depend on money and whether my man is tired of listenin to me complainin about all the things we ain't got. That ain't right."

"How you gonna live in this world without dependin on money?"

"I'm gonna live in this world without dependin on *nobody*. Nobody but myself. If I have to work a job then I'm gonna do it, but I'm gonna work the job, the job ain't gonna work me. If I find a man who wants to do what I want to do, and he wants to do it with me, then we can do it together. He'll help me only cause it's something that we both want to do together. But if *I* want a job and if *I* want to go to school and if *I* want a baby *I'm* gonna have to find some way to do it. Those things are *not* wrong to want. I'll never believe they are no matter how old I get.

"Me and Danny was talkin about that, about havin to live in a world that don't make no sense. Livin in a world where a person gets hungry and there is food around and he's able to earn his food but still he can't eat. About two people lovin each other and people sayin they can't touch each other cause you ain't got enough money in your piggy bank to get an abortion or raise a child. We decided and we know that it's true that there ain't nothin wrong with sex—there ain't nothin wrong with lovin somebody—it's just that you have to defend yourself against all the supidity in the world and realize that the *world* is screwed up, not you. I'm gonna defend myself by waitin till I can give my child the things I want easily before I have one. I'm gonna wait till I go to school and wait till I live with a good man that wants what I want and will help me get it.

"I'm gonna defend myself against this sick world by taking my birth-control pills every day or sticking some weird rubber thing up my crotch every time I get the hots. But I'm always gonna realize that it's *them* that's wrong and *not me*. I'm not sick and neither is Danny. And I love him and I hope you hurry up and take me to the doctor's and get me some damn pills so we can be together before he leaves me. . . ." I had begun talkin loud and almost screamin at Moma. Tears were runnin down my face.

"Oh, I'm sorry, Moma, I'm sorry." I burst out cryin, then ran to my room.

Later Moma came in and sat on the bed. She rested my head on her lap and stroked my head.

"Moma understands. I don't agree with a lot of the things you said, but you'll have time to get it together, Marcia. I hope and pray you do. You know Moma loves you. We'll go to the doctor's soon. And everythin's gonna be okay. Now come on in the kitchen and have some dinner with me, okay?"

"Yes, Ma."

A couple a days passed. I was bein my old self again and feelin all right, sort of. It seems Danny and Evette were only hangin out together for a couple of days. (I knew Evette couldn't handle it.) But I didn't feel bad about it. I guess Danny had to get somethin off his chest, well not his chest but, well, you know what I'm tryin to say, well, I guess he did it with Evette. I don't hate her either, no more than I did. Maybe she did somethin I didn't have the guts to do. I don't know. I just know, I wish me and Danny could have did what's gonna happen anyway, together, and I wish all of this didn't happen. And I wish things could be the way they used to be.

I didn't see Danny for at least a week. He just didn't come around, and as I was walkin up to the store I saw Danny in the window. I didn't want to go in and have us be cold to each other, but I couldn't get around it. I mean we were being adult about the whole thing. It was just gettin worse. And I don't know what I'd do if Danny decided to leave me for good. Okay, let me get myself together and get these clothes out. I walked in and went up to the counter where he was standin.

The man was bringin out his stuff. Danny handed him the money and walked right out. He didn't turn around once. I said to myself, "Well, that's it. Danny don't want me no more. Well, I guess I don't blame him. It's all over, just like that." I felt tears wellin up in my eyes. But I held it in. I got my clothes. He didn't even say hello. I mean, I knew he saw me.

I walked out and there he was, standin at the end of the block, waitin. Maybe he wasn't waitin. Maybe . . . I don't know. I tried to be cool and hold back the tears. When I got up to where he was standin, he came up to me.

"Hello, how are you, Marcia Anne?
I'd like to walk you home if I can."
A couple minutes later we was holdin hands.
And he told me I was still his dream,
While sharin a cone of chocolate ice cream.
And one day when we was all alone.
I let it happen on my own.